Ricky, Rocky, and Ringo
GO TO THE
MOON
by MAURI KUNNAS

CROWN PUBLISHERS, INC.   NEW YORK

Early one morning, Captain Tim of Space
Control called for Ricky, Rocky, and Ringo.
Zack, the oldest and most important robot-
scientist on the moon, had stopped working.
"We need your help, boys!" said Captain Tim.
"You must fly up to the moon and see what's
wrong with Zack!"

"TEN, NINE, EIGHT...!!!" But before they hit "BLAST OFF!!!" Ricky's mother ran on to the launch pad. "STOP!!!" she cried.
"You boys aren't going anywhere without proper woolen scarfs, hats, and mittens! It's cold on the moon."

Ricky grumbled, but Mother said, "You'll find these things very useful, you'll see!"
" ... SEVEN, SIX, FIVE, FOUR, THREE, TWO, ONE, BLAST OFF!!!"

Finally, Ricky, Rocky,
and Ringo were on
their way.
"Mother always forgets
that our space suits
keep us warm." Ricky
laughed. "Look!"
shouted Rocky. "There
goes the booster rocket!
Moon, here we come!"

SO LONG
ROBOT

But suddenly, they all began to
float around!
"Oh, no!" said Rocky. "We forgot we are
weightless in space!"

"I should have known Mother's scarfs would cause nothing but trouble up here," Ricky said. "Now I can't find our magnetic boots!"

Soon the boys forgot their troubles.
The view was beautiful.
"Let's have a little space walk before lunch,"
Ringo said. They put on their space packs
and zoomed outside.

LUNCH TIME!
Eating in outer space is very tricky.
"Hamburger!! Table!! Come back here at
once!! Who took my
cocoa?" cried Ricky.

At long last, Ricky, Rocky, and Ringo
landed on the moon. They peeked out
the rocket window, searching for Zack.
Lots of the robots were bright and colorful.
"Don't they all look great?" asked Ricky.

Rocky jumped from crater to crater.
"There's good old Zack! Ringo!"
Rocky called. "Stop trying to
impress those new robots.
Come here and help!"

"What's wrong, Zack?" Rocky asked.
"I feel bad next to those new robots." Zack
sighed. "They all look so colorful and I'm
so plain." "I can't cure sadness with a
screwdriver, and that's all Captain Tim gave
us," said Ringo. That gave Ricky an idea.

"OH, MY!! WHAT BEAUTIFUL COLORS!!"
cried Zack. "Would you like them?" Ricky aske
"Now no one can make you
feel plain!"
The boys laughed.

"Good-bye, Zack!"
"Thank you, Ricky, Rocky, and Ringo!" called Zack.

Ricky's mother wasn't surprised when she heard about everything that had happened. "Didn't Mama tell you that scarfs, hats, and mittens would be useful on the moon?"

Library of Congress Cataloging-in-Publication Data.

Kunnas, Mauri. Ricky, Rocky, and Ringo go to the moon. Summary: The misadventures of Ricky, Rocky, and Ringo as they fly their rocket ship to the moon to find out why Zack the robot isn't working. [1. Science Fiction. 2. Humorous Stories] I. Title. II. Series.
PZ7.K9492Rg 1986   [E]   86-2324

ISBN 0-517-56232-4
10 9 8 7 6 5 4 3 2 1
First Edition